To Tommy and Becky,
    May this book bring
you joy especially with the "wee"
    Sternals that may appear.....

SARAH'S BEAD

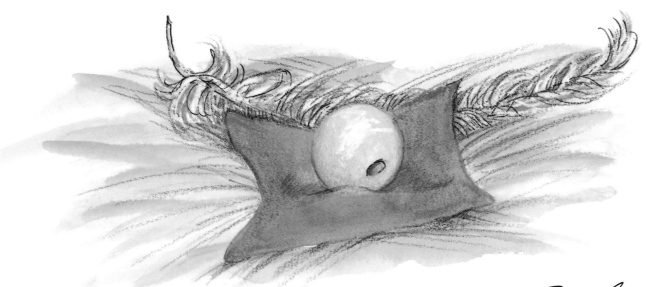

Caroline S. Garrett
2000

Love, Caroline

Dedication
For Mother, Dad and my family: Waddy, Connie, Ben, Sally and dear sister Sue.
With special thanks to Pat for her help with this book and to Charlie.
Thank you all for the Light you've given me. *CSG*

Text and illustrations copyright © 2000 by Caroline S. Garrett

Published by Divine Mirror Press
An imprint of IAM Spirit PUBLISHING
A division of Remington Literary Associates, Inc.
10131 Coors Rd. NW, Ste. l 2-886, Albuquerque, New Mexico 87114

Illustrations done in Winsor and Newton watercolor, ink and Prismacolor pencils on Arches 110-pound hot press paper
Color separation and prepress services by COLORCORP, INC., Colorado, USA.
Text set in Adobe Garamond by Wiatt's Design, Richmond, Virginia.

Printed in Hong Kong by Midas Printing Ltd.

First Edition
SAN: 253–1607

Publisher's Cataloging-in-Publication
(Provided by Quality Books, Inc.)

Garrett, Caroline S.
    Sarah's Bead / by Caroline S. Garrett. -- 1st ed.
    p. cm.
    SUMMARY: Sarah, a pack rat, discovers a bead that
becomes her prize possession. The birth of a very
special baby "king" in the stable where Sarah lives
makes her realize that she is willing to give away her
precious possession in response to his love, for the
baby is Jesus Christ.
    LCCN: 00-100891
    ISBN: 0-9678780-8-X
    1. Jesus Christ--Nativity--Juvenile fiction.   2. Wood
rats--Juvenile fiction.   I. Title.

PZ7.G2116Sar 2000   [E]
                    QB100-267

SARAH'S BEAD
by Caroline S. Garrett

DIVINE MIRROR PRESS
Albuquerque, New Mexico

Sarah, the packrat, lived in a stable beside an inn. Often, she sneaked inside the inn after the guests went to bed. Before the kind innkeeper cleaned up, Sarah would search under the tables for treasures. Whatever she found she pushed in her carrying pouch. Once she discovered a coin. Other times, she found an ivory needle, a feather, patches of cloth, bits of leather, and a dead insect.

One night, as a sandstorm roared, Sarah started to run back to her warm nest empty-handed, when she stumbled over an object, sending her head-over-tail.

A beautiful bead lay under a table, near the innkeeper's foot. She stashed

the bead in her pouch and dashed for the stable.

"Look at what I found! Isn't it beautiful?" Her stable mates agreed. Truly, the bead was Sarah's best find ever.

She scrambled to the loft. Grabbing some cloth, she rubbed the bead until it shone. Then she held it to her cheek. "I'll never let this bead go!"

Feeling proud, Sarah wrapped it in more regal-looking cloth and kept it next to her while she slept.

Later, noises awakened Sarah. She peeked through the cracks. Outside, the sand still blew. Travelers overflowed the streets, looking for shelter.

"It's a good thing I found the bead. I would hate to think of what might happen to it under that crowd of feet."

Sarah noticed that the innkeeper broke through the crowd. He cleared a path for a man and a young woman. Then the stable door squeaked. Sarah scampered across the loft and peered down.

"You and your wife can sleep here," the innkeeper said.

He helped the man seat the very weary looking young woman. After the innkeeper left, Sarah watched the couple. Often, people came to the stable to take out the ox or the donkey or to milk the goat but never to sleep. The other animals dozed off again but not Sarah.

The man and woman whispered. Sarah couldn't hear what they said, but she knew something was happening. Something important. Soon she heard a cry.

A baby! Sarah could hardly believe it. A baby had been born, right here, in her stable! The mother wrapped the baby in a binding cloth, making it snug and warm. Yawning, Sarah returned to her nest. This night had been full of surprises.

The next day when Sarah awoke, she remembered her bead. She felt more proud of her special treasure than ever.

Suddenly, voices reminded her of the baby. She dashed out of her nest to peek.

New visitors had arrived. A shepherd knelt before the ox's manger, which served as a cradle.

"Is this the new king?" the shepherd asked.

"Yes," the husband answered, smiling.

King? Sarah wondered. *What king?*

"We brought a small gift." The shepherd held out a little blanket. The mother laid it over the baby. "My wife is a good weaver, and this is the best blanket she has ever made. We wanted our new king to have it."

Sarah thought the baby's birth was a wonderful thing, but a king born in a stable? After the shepherds left, Sarah wanted a closer look at this baby king. A thought stopped her.

I am a packrat. And people are afraid of us… uh, rodents.

Below, the baby gurgled. "How could a king be afraid of me?" Sarah whispered to herself. "I am little and harmless and not scary at all."

To prove it, she raced to her bead.

Gazing at its polished surface, Sarah said, "Hello, baby king! I am Sarah." In her reflection, her whiskers twitched. Sadly, Sarah admitted, "I do look scary. My whiskers are too long. And they go up and down when I speak." She quickly plucked out a few whiskers, which made her cheeks swell, adding to what she already felt must be a very frightening face. Meeting the baby king was going to be difficult with his family standing guard. "I will scare them too," Sarah cried miserably.

As the days passed, Sarah sadly watched from above as the baby king grew. Her wish to meet him grew too. Yet Sarah believed his family would never see her as the harmless little friend she so much wanted to be.

The other animals offered little encouragement and said, "People don't like little rats anymore than they like big ones."

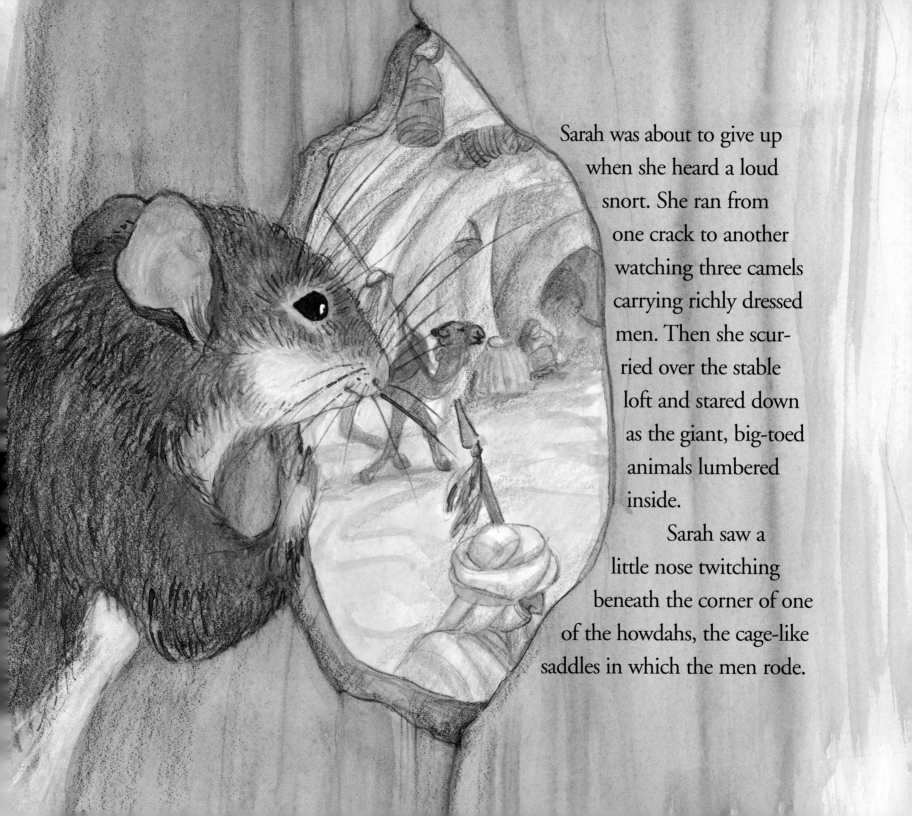

Sarah was about to give up when she heard a loud snort. She ran from one crack to another watching three camels carrying richly dressed men. Then she scurried over the stable loft and stared down as the giant, big-toed animals lumbered inside.

Sarah saw a little nose twitching beneath the corner of one of the howdahs, the cage-like saddles in which the men rode.

While the camels sat and the turbaned men admired the baby, Sarah whispered to the hiding guest, "Who are you?"

"I am Abel." He scampered up to Sarah's loft. "I have come to honor the great king."

"YOU are visiting the king?" Sarah asked.

"Of course." Abel smiled. "Here's my gift." He held up a long golden thread.

Sarah gasped. "How beautiful!" Secretly, she wished she could add it to her treasure collection.

"What did you give the king?" Abel asked.

"I, uh . . ." Sarah sputtered. She'd never thought of giving the little king a gift. "I . . . I haven't decided. But I am sure I have something perfect. Perhaps you might help me choose."

Sarah brought out a few things. "How about this?" She held out her feather.

"It'll make him sneeze."

"A needle then?"

"Too dangerous. Babies can't have tiny things around. They stick them in their mouths."

"Oh," said Sarah, feeling a bit silly. She picked through her things. "A piece of leather? His mother could sew it on his clothes."

Abel shook his head. "Not special enough."

"A patch of lion's fur then?"

Sarah rushed into her

nest and came back with a matted bit of fluff.

"Are you sure it's genuine lion?" Abel looked closely, doubt in his eyes.

Sarah was getting nervous. She realized she had only one thing left — the one thing she could not possibly give away.

The camels groaned. Abel rushed to the edge of the loft. "I have to go."

Sarah gasped. "Now? But you just got —"

"The wise men said we could not stay long. Promise me you'll give the baby king my gift." Abel held out the shining thread.

"But I … I …"

"Please promise," Abel begged. "This is a very special thread from great King David's robe. My ancestors have guarded it for many many years. It will bring a miracle." Abel thrust his gift in Sarah's paws and leapt for the last camel as it swayed out of the door.

Sarah held her breath, but Abel landed on his feet. He silently mouthed,

"Remember your promise," before he scurried back under the howdah.

Sarah's paws trembled. She'd never held any-thing so beautiful — except her bead. She rushed into her nest.

"Oh! They are so lovely together." She grabbed her ivory needle and threaded the golden treasure through the bead. "Perfect!" Sarah sighed, knowing she would look like royalty herself wearing this necklace.

Remember your promise. Sarah frowned at the thought. She had not really promised. In Abel's rush, he'd only thought she had. She gently wrapped the necklace in a patch of cloth, tucked it beside her, and closed her eyes.

That night, Sarah dreamed she tied Abel's golden thread around the baby king's wrist, but the mother woke and screamed. The man caught Sarah by the tail and threw her into a sand-storm. Sarah awoke, shuddering. Then she became angry with herself.

"Enough of your quaking, Sarah! You must do it. Abel must have his miracle."

Below, everyone slept soundly. Hoping to get this over with fast, Sarah grabbed the cloth that held the necklace and shot down a post. She raced on tiptoe to the manger and scrambled into the straw.

Scurrying beneath the warm blanket beside the bundled babe, Sarah opened the cloth. She was about to slip her precious bead from the thread when the baby sighed. Sarah glanced up. What she saw shocked her.

His face was the most beautiful thing Sarah had ever seen. He blinked at Sarah. Her heart started pounding. Oh, no! He'd seen her ugly, whiskery face. She told her feet to move, but nothing happened. The baby king blinked again. Then his cheeks twitched. Sarah's throat began to hurt. Tears rushed into her eyes. She knew she was going to start bawling too.

Then he… smiled.

Sarah felt stunned. His smile grew bigger. Tears washed down Sarah's face, but not from sadness. Joy filled her!

Carefully, she wrapped the golden thread with her precious bead around His little wrist.

Remembering Abel's warning about babies and small things, she made a tight knot. The baby waved his hands in the air and cooed.

Sarah squeaked, her heart over-flowing with love.

"Joseph, wake up! There's a rat in the manger!"

"Oh, no!" Sarah ran for her life. As she disappeared under the manger, the man swept a hand beneath it and caught her. Sarah trembled.

"Wait!" the mother cautioned as the man rose to his feet.

"Mary, I was just going to throw—"

"Look," his wife pointed. "What is that on the baby's wrist?"

"A bracelet," Joseph whispered in wonder. "It… it seems to be glowing."

Sarah stopped wiggling to look. *Yes, beautiful rainbow colors streamed from the bead!* The baby king glanced right at her and flapped his little hands above his head. The woman said, "Joseph, I … I think the rat must have

given this amazing bracelet to the child."

"But Mary, it's only a ra—"
The man went silent as the child laughed and waved his arms.
"See how he loves it," Mary bade her husband. "Bring the animal closer."
Joseph gently cupped Sarah in his hands, and she did not try to scamper away. The baby reached toward Sarah. he touched her soft fur. Sarah tingled all over. It was the best feeling she'd ever felt.

The bead glowed even brighter. The thread gleamed too, shining more than Sarah had ever noticed before. The light grew and grew until Sarah

saw angels around the manger. Their
shimmering light flooded the stable.

"A miracle!" Sarah said in awe.
Oh, how she wished Abel were here.
She gazed at the Baby King, and her
heart melted at His sweet smile. The
sight of the angels was glorious indeed,
but for Sarah, the biggest miracle was
knowing the Baby King loved her!

In her small, pure voice she sang
with the angels for the whole world
to hear:

Caroline S. Garrett

Come see our Baby King!
Come see the light Love brings!
A friend to all, both great and small,
This Baby beauty bright
Has come — Oh, King of Light!